GROSSET & DUNLAP
Published by the Penguin Group
Penguin Group (USA) Inc., 375 Hudson Street, New York, New York 10014, U.S.A.
Penguin Group (Canada), 10 Alcorn Avenue, Toronto, Ontario, Canada M4V 3B2
(a division of Pearson Penguin Canada Inc.)
Penguin Books Ltd, 80 Strand, London WC2R 0RL, England
Penguin Ireland, 25 St Stephen's Green, Dublin 2, Ireland
(a division of Penguin Books Ltd)
Penguin Group (Australia), 250 Camberwell Road, Camberwell, Victoria 3124, Australia
(a division of Pearson Australia Group Pty Ltd)
Penguin Books India Pvt Ltd, 11 Community Centre, Panchsheel Park, New Delhi - 110 017, India
Penguin Group (NZ), Cnr Airborne and Rosedale Roads, Albany, Auckland 1310, New Zealand
(a division of Pearson New Zealand Ltd)
Penguin Books (South Africa) (Pty) Ltd, 24 Sturdee Avenue, Rosebank, Johannesburg 2196, South Africa

Penguin Books Ltd, Registered Offices:
80 Strand, London WC2R 0RL, England

Library of Congress Cataloging-in-Publication Data

Bryant, Megan E.
Cinderella / by Megan E. Bryant ; illustrated by Scott Neely.
p. cm. — (Berry fairy tales)
"Strawberry Shortcake."
Summary: An adaptation of the traditional tale of Cinderella, featuring Strawberry
Shortcake and her friends as the various characters, in which a sweet girl and her wicked
stepsisters each hope the Prince will choose her to be Berry Princess.
ISBN 0-448-43979-4
[1. Fairy tales. 2. Folklore—France.] I. Neely, Scott, ill. II. Cinderella. English. III.
Title. IV. Series.
PZ8.B8425Ci 2005
398.2'0944'02—dc22
2005003381

ISBN 0-448-43979-4   10 9 8 7 6 5 4 3 2 1

Berry Fairy Tales

Cinderella

By Megan E. Bryant
Illustrated by Scott Neely

Grosset & Dunlap

Once upon a time, Strawberry Shortcake and her berry best friends went over to Blueberry Muffin's house.

"Let's play dress-up and act out a story," Angel Cake suggested. "What about Cinderella?"

"That's my berry favorite fairy tale!" exclaimed Strawberry.

"But how can we play Cinderella?" asked Ginger Snap. "We don't have a castle or a coach or anything!"

"Don't worry, Ginger," Strawberry replied as the girls put on their costumes. "All you have to do is use your imagination!" She took a deep breath. "In a kingdom far, far away . . ."

. . . there lived a berry sweet girl named Cinderella. She was kind to everyone—even to her wicked stepmother and stepsisters, who weren't very nice at all!

"Cinderella, have you scrubbed the floors, beat the rugs, cleaned the kitchen, washed the clothes, fed the pets, watered the flowers, and weeded the berry patch?" asked her stepmother at breakfast one bright morning.

"Not yet, dear Stepmother, but I will!" said Cinderella cheerfully.

Just then, there was a loud knock at the door. Cinderella ran to answer it.

"Hear ye, hear ye! His Royal Highness Prince Charming is hosting a ball tonight to find the next Berry Princess to tend the royal berry patch. The entire kingdom is invited, and all young ladies are required to attend!" announced a royal page.

Cinderella's stepsisters squealed. "How berry exciting! I hope the Prince picks me! I want to live in the palace!"

"Me, too!" exclaimed Cinderella. "I would take good care of the royal berry crop and help it grow better every day!"

"Just a minute, Cinderella," her stepmother said. "Who said you could go?"

"But—the royal page said that the entire kingdom is invited!" Cinderella said. "And every young lady—"

"All right, all right," Cinderella's stepmother replied with a nasty smile. "You can go—but if, and only if, you finish your chores. All of your chores."

"I'll work berry hard!" exclaimed Cinderella. "Thank you, Stepmother!"

In truth, though, the wicked stepmother had no intention of letting Cinderella go to the ball. Cinderella had a gift for growing the best berry crop. Her stepmother knew that the Prince would never pick one of her own daughters to be the Berry Princess if he knew about Cinderella.

So she kept Cinderella busier than ever!

"Cinderella! Fix my hair!" barked her stepmother.

"Cinderella! Mend my dress!" ordered her stepsister.

"Cinderella! Polish my shoes!" snapped her other stepsister.

Cinderella's stepmother and stepsisters kept her so busy that before she knew it, the clock was chiming six—and she hadn't finished any of her chores!

In a flurry of petticoats and ribbons, Cinderella's stepsisters and stepmother hurried off to the ball, leaving poor Cinderella home alone.

"I wish I could have gone to the ball, too," she said quietly. A single tear slipped down her cheek and landed right on a plump, red strawberry. Suddenly, the strawberry began to grow bigger and bigger, until it was the size of a coach!

"Why are you crying, my dear?" asked a beautiful lady as she stepped out of the strawberry coach. "I'm your Berry Godmother, and I've come to send you to the ball!"

"Send *me* to the ball?" Cinderella asked.

"Of course!" replied her Berry Godmother. "No one in all of Strawberry-land loves berries as much as you do. But how can the Prince pick you to be the new Berry Princess if you don't even go to the Berry Ball?"

"But I can't go to the Berry Ball," Cinderella said sadly. "I don't have anything to wear, and no way to get there."

Her Berry Godmother winked. With a wave of her berry wand, strawberry sparkles filled the air—and Cinderella found herself dressed like a beautiful princess!

"Thank you so berry much!" exclaimed Cinderella as she twirled around.

"You're welcome, my dear. But remember to be home before the clock strikes midnight—or all the magic will disappear!"

"I will," promised Cinderella. And she got into the coach and hurried off to the ball.

Before long, Cinderella arrived at the palace. It was the most beautiful place she had ever seen! Tall turrets gleamed against the night sky as tiny berry lights twinkled like little stars. A royal page hurried over to her carriage.

"Welcome, my lady," announced the page. "Prince Charming is receiving guests in the grand ballroom!"

Cinderella slowly walked up the wide staircase, her heart fluttering as she started to feel shy. As she stepped into the ballroom, Cinderella felt someone tap her shoulder.

It was the Prince! "Would you like to dance?" he asked.

"Oh, yes—berry much!" she replied.

When the dance was finished, Prince Charming took Cinderella on a walk through the castle berry patch as the stars twinkled overhead.

"I've never seen such a wonderful berry patch!" Cinderella exclaimed.

"These berries need a special person to look after them," the Prince replied. "I think—"

Suddenly, the old clock started to chime.

"It's midnight already?" gasped Cinderella. "I'm going to be berry late! I've got to go!" She spun around and raced down the palace steps.

"Wait! I don't even know your name!" yelled the Prince.

But it was too late. Cinderella had already disappeared into the night.

Cinderella was almost home when the last stroke of midnight
was heard through the land. Her coach, her gown, everything
had disappeared—except for one shiny strawberry slipper.

"That's berry strange," Cinderella said. "I must have lost my
other shoe when I ran away from the palace."

Cinderella hurried home in her tattered dress and bare feet, carefully carrying her strawberry shoe. She slipped the shoe under her pillow, tucked into bed, and fell asleep with a smile still on her face.

The sun was shining brightly the next morning when Cinderella awoke. "Going to the ball was like a dream come true!" she whispered. "I'm so glad I have my shoe to remind me that it really happened."

Downstairs, Cinderella was busy making breakfast when her sleepy
stepsisters and stepmother wandered into the kitchen, yawning loudly.

"Good morning!" Cinderella said cheerfully. "How was the ball?"

"Too bad you couldn't have been there," one of her stepsisters replied.
"It was quite scandalous! The Prince spent all his time with a strange
young lady no one had ever seen before. Then she ran off into the night!"

"How berry odd," Cinderella said as she smiled to herself.

There was a loud knock at the door. "Cinderella, go answer the door!" ordered her stepmother.

To Cinderella's surprise, it was the royal page, with an entourage from the castle!

"By decree of His Royal Highness Prince Charming, all young ladies in the kingdom must try on this shoe," announced the page. "Whoever it fits will become the next Berry Princess!"

"Stay in the kitchen," Cinderella's stepmother hissed. "Don't come out until I call you." She pushed Cinderella through the kitchen doors—just as the Prince entered the cottage!

The page tried to fit the shoe on one of the stepsisters—but her foot was way too long. Then he tried to fit the shoe on the other stepsister—but her foot was way too wide.

"Aren't there any other young ladies here?" asked Prince Charming sadly. "We've tried every other house in the kingdom!"

"What about the young lady who answers the door?" asked the page.

"That's nobody!" replied the stepmother. "Just Cinderella—and she didn't go to the ball!"

Hearing her name, Cinderella burst out of the kitchen. "Yes, I did!" she said. "And I would like to try on the shoe, please!"

It fit perfectly! Cinderella showed the Prince her other strawberry slipper.
"You're the one!" Prince Charming exclaimed. "Cinderella, will you be my
Berry Princess and help tend all the strawberries in the land?"
"I'd like that berry much!" replied Cinderella.
And they lived berry happily ever after!